Words to Know Before You Read

animal

bring

brought

crackers

disaster

people

popcorn

pretzels

spilled

www.rourkeeducationalmedia.com

Edited by Luana Mitten
Illustrated by Anita DuFalla
Art Direction and Page Layout by Renee Brady

Library of Congress Cataloging-in-Publication Data

Robertson, J. Jean
 Disaster on the 100th day / J. Jean Robertson.
     p. cm. -- (Little Birdie Books)
 ISBN 978-1-61741-799-3 (hard cover - English) (alk. paper)
 ISBN 978-1-61236-003-4 (soft cover - English)
 ISBN 978-1-61236-716-3 (e-Book - English)
 ISBN 978-1-63430-340-8 (hard cover - Spanish)
 ISBN 978-1-61810-522-6 (soft cover - Spanish)
 ISBN 978-1-62169-014-6 (e-Book - Spanish)
 Library of Congress Control Number: 2011924609

*Scan for Related Titles
and Teacher Resources*

Also Available as:

Rourke Educational Media
Printed in the United States of America,
North Mankato, Minnesota

Rourke
Educational Media

rourkeeducationalmedia.com

customerservice@rourkeeducationalmedia.com • PO Box 643328 Vero Beach, Florida 32964

DISASTER
on the 100th Day

By J. Jean Robertson

Illustrated by Anita DuFalla

Look! See what Zoe Zebra brought for our 100th day party.

4

Animal stickers!

Guess what Rafi Rabbit brought

Carrots, of course.

Did Ella Elephant bring that pile of peanuts?

Popcorn!

10

Lily Lion
brought popcorn.

Parker Parrot
brought crackers.

People crackers!

More food? Tyler Tiger brought pretzels.

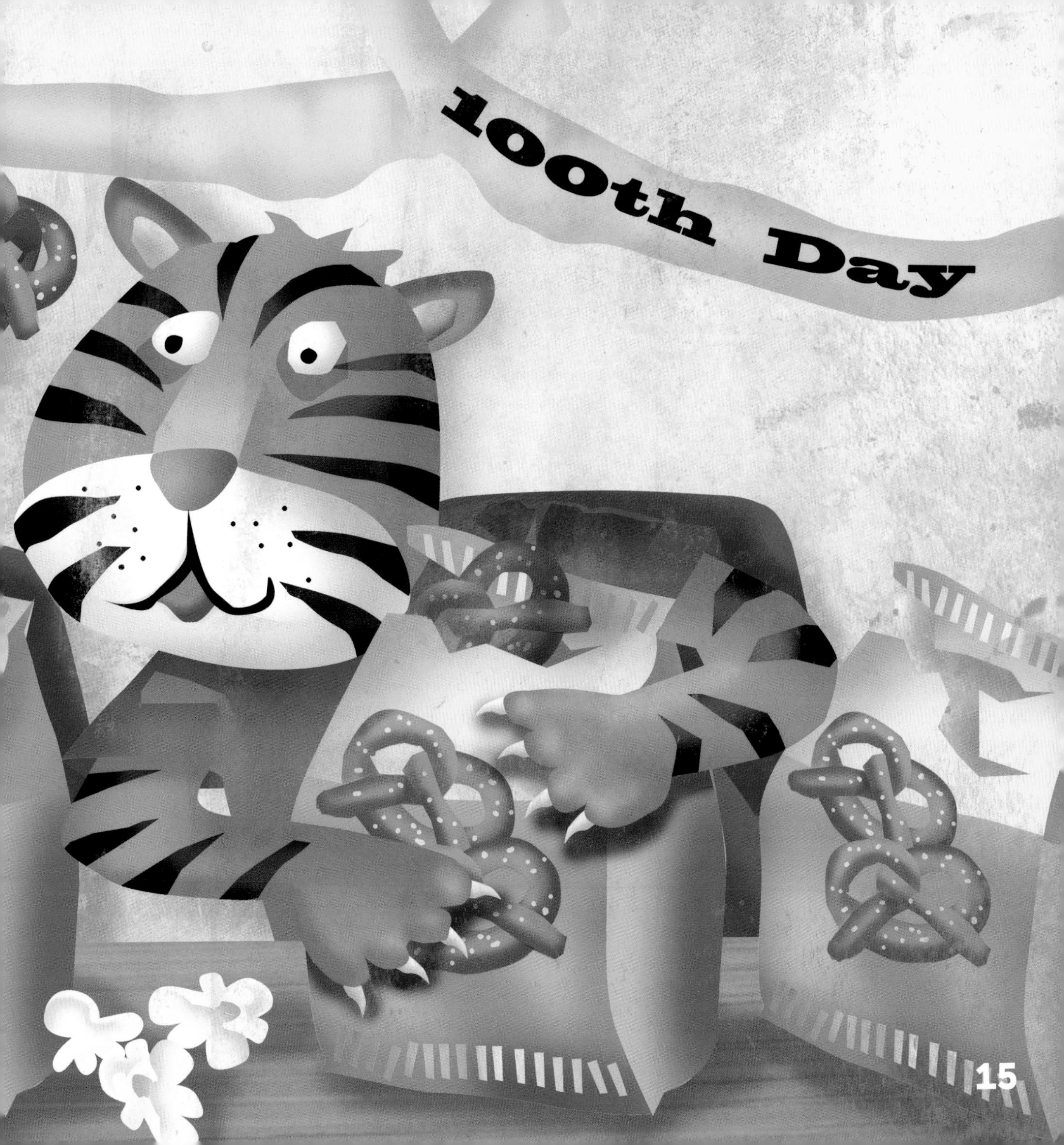
100th Day

What will we drink?

David Duck brought 100 bottles of water.

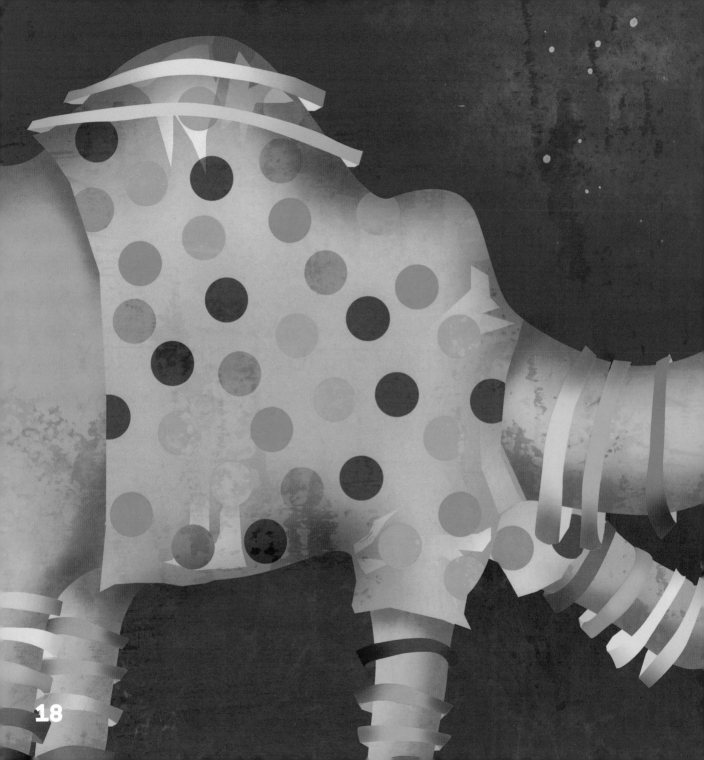

We can wear these animal
bands Cadee Camel brought.

Mike Monkey spilled all his marbles.

What a disaster. One hundred marbles all over the floor!

After Reading Activities

You and the Story...

What was the disaster on the 100th day?

Which animal caused the disaster on the 100th day?

What would you bring to share at a 100th day party?

Tell a friend about how you would celebrate the 100th Day of School.

Words You Know Now...

Each word is missing a vowel. Can you write the words on a piece of paper and add the missing vowel?

an_mal   peopl_

br_ng   popc_rn

br_ught   pr_tzels

crack_rs   spill_d

disast_r

You Could...Plan a Party for the 100th Day

- Use a calendar to find out what day is the 100th Day of School.

- Make invitations inviting another class, your parents, or the principal to come to your party. Make sure the invitations tell:
    - What the party is for
    - What your guests need to bring (a collection of 100 things)
    - The date and time of the party
    - The place the party will be at

- Plan what you will do at the party.
    - How will you count to 100?
    - Is there a song you could sing at the party?
    - How will your guests share their collections?

- Make a list of what supplies you need for the party.

- Be sure to think about how you can keep from having a disaster at YOUR party!

About the Author

J. Jean Robertson, also known as Bushka to her grandchildren and many other kids, lives in San Antonio, Florida with her husband. She is retired after many years of teaching. She loves to read, travel, and write books for children.

Meet The Author!
www.meetREMauthors.com

About the Illustrator

Acclaimed for its versatility in style, Anita DuFalla's work has appeared in many educational books, newspaper articles, and business advertisements and on numerous posters, book and magazine covers, and even giftwraps. Anita's passion for pattern is evident in both her artwork and her collection of 400 patterned tights. She lives in the Friendship neighborhood of Pittsburgh, Pennsylvania with her son, Lucas.